THE HOUSE ON THE HILL

MILDRED MASTERS

The House on the Hill

SCHOLASTIC INC.
New York Toronto London Auckland Sydney Tokyo

ISBN 0-590-32894-8

Copyright © 1979, 1982, by Mildred Carolyn Masters. This edition published by Scholastic Inc., 730 Broadway, New York, N.Y. 10003, by arrangement with Greenwillow Books, a division of William Morrow and Co., Inc.

12 11 10 9 8 7 6 5 4 3 2 1   9   3 4 5 6 7/8

Printed in the U.S.A.   10

To my sons and to my sisters

The day after Jenny Reed finished fourth grade, her best friend, Mary Ellen, drove off with all of her family in their red station wagon. They weren't ever coming back. Mary Ellen's father had a new job, and it was far away in Nebraska.

Jenny could see Mary Ellen in the back seat, with her two brothers and a lot of pillows and blankets. She didn't look up, and she didn't wave. Jenny knew that it was because she didn't want to move away, and she didn't want anyone to see her cry. Jenny cried though, and so did her mother.

For as long as Jenny could remember, Mary Ellen had lived around the corner from her. They had gone to school together, played together, and talked everything over. Jenny stayed with Mary Ellen's family when Mrs. Reed was in the hospital, and Mary Ellen's house was another place where she felt at home. Now all of that was gone.

Jenny was ten, and she lived in the town of

Crooked Creek in southern Indiana. Crooked Creek didn't have a movie theater or a big department store or a swimming pool, but in spite of that, it was a lively place. People from far and near visited there because of the beautiful countryside, the fine old buildings, and the interesting shops.

Many of the people of Crooked Creek sold things which they made themselves—things like hand-made furniture and clothing, baskets, and quilts. Paints and brushes and other artists' supplies were for sale in a lot of stores, too, because a lot of artists lived there, and many others came to stay for a few weeks or a few months.

Some of the out-of-town people spent the whole summer, in houses they owned on the north edge of town. The houses were pretty, set back from the road and surrounded by a lot of land, but most of them had Keep Out signs, too, and Jenny didn't know any of the children who stayed in them.

Jenny had always loved Crooked Creek, but without Mary Ellen, everything was going to be different. Her school was only two blocks from home, on the edge of town, but now, vacation time, the empty swings on the playground looked lonely. Most of the kids Jenny went to school with lived on farms, and some of them rode the bus for an hour or more to get there. Mary Ellen's mother or father used to drive them out to one of the farms sometimes. Now, since she and her mother didn't have a car, Jenny wouldn't be able to see much of the farm kids during the summer.

Hilary and Ellery Aldrich were the only kids who lived near Jenny. Hilary was almost thirteen and spent most of her time reading magazines and fussing with her clothes. Ellery was seven. He could be fun, but a lot of the time, he was a pest.

Even Jenny's sister, Linda, who had just finished her first year at Indiana University, had decided to stay at college for the summer. She had a good job there and wanted to take some summer courses. Before Linda went away to college, the phone was always ringing, and her friends were in and out. It was crowded at home, and there were a lot of arguments, but it was fun, too. Now it was quiet all the time. It seemed to Jenny that the summer was going to be a mess.

(2)

Genevieve's Restaurant on Main Street was the center of things and Genevieve was a very important person in Crooked Creek. At Genevieve's, you found out what was happening in town, and sooner or later you saw just about everybody who lived there. Genevieve had the news about new babies, and she knew who was sick, who was moving, and who was looking for a job. The out-of-town buses stopped there, and Crooked Creek's one taxi was parked outside when it wasn't on call. Some people, including Genevieve herself, said the whole town would go to pieces without her.

It was true that many of the tourists went instead to the Indiana Inn just down the street. At the Inn, there were red tablecloths and glasses with long stems, and the waitresses wore long dresses and ruffled aprons. Before Jenny's sister Linda went away to college, she had worked there. She didn't like it very much, but Jenny always liked seeing her go to work in her pretty long dress.

Hilary and Ellery Aldrich and their parents went to the Indiana Inn a lot, but most of the Crooked Creek people went to Genevieve's. There were no tablecloths at Genevieve's, and instead of pretty waitresses in long dresses, there were short plump Genevieve and her twin sons, who helped her run the place. Louise, who did the cooking, stayed in the kitchen because she was bashful. Jenny often helped out at the restaurant, just for some company and something to do. She set tables and filled water glasses and cleared away. Then Genevieve gave her a cool drink and a cookie, and if the place wasn't too busy, they talked for a while.

One afternoon when Jenny was at the restaurant, there was a quiet spell, and she and Genevieve sat down at the counter with glasses of lemonade.

"I got a letter from Mary Ellen," Jenny said. Genevieve missed Mary Ellen, too.

"She says the people in Nebraska are nice, but not as nice as us. She says their house is brand-new and bigger than their house here. She says her school is right on the corner. She says it gets just as hot there as it does here. And it's flat. No hills."

"How could a person go and live so far away from Crooked Creek?" Genevieve asked. "But then, it's a good job for her dad. They'll have a fine life there."

"I wish Mary Ellen would come back!" Jenny said. "I haven't got anybody to talk to at all."

"What do you mean? You've got the whole town to talk to. You come in here every day and talk to them!"

"The whole town isn't my age."

"What about Hilary Aldrich? She's only a year or two older, and she lives near you."

"Oh, you know what Hilary's like, Genevieve. She's always picking people apart. I feel so stupid around her. Anyway, she's going to boarding school next fall, so she won't be around at all. And Ellery's okay, but he's just a little kid. Besides, the two of them will be going to camp soon, and they'll stay almost till school starts."

"I see what you mean," Genevieve said. "Most of the kids your age live on the north end of town, don't they? It's too bad they took the bus off. You could have gotten over there easy if it was still running. Anyway, I sure am glad of your company, I know that. And maybe you'll make some new friends before the summer's over." Then Genevieve had to get back to work. Jenny sat there looking at her empty lemonade glass for a while, and then she decided it was time to leave.

"On your way home, will you take Willy Rudolf his iced tea?" Genevieve asked. "He's too busy to come in, with so many tourists in town." She put a large paper cup of iced tea and the two biggest cookies she could find in a paper bag and gave them to Jenny.

(3)

Mr. Willy Rudolf, who was tremendously old and cheerful, sat every day in a canvas chair on the sidewalk between the Crooked Creek Art Center and the laundromat. He always wore his straw hat because the Indiana sun was hot, and Mr. Rudolf didn't have much hair left to protect the top of his head.

One of Mr. Rudolf's jobs was to get tourists into the Art Center. There his great-nephew Dave would sketch or paint them for a very reasonable price. The Art Center was a two-story building with a huge window in front, and in that window Dave sat and sketched while people watched. Mr. Rudolf also kept an eye on the laundromat, a very busy place which Dave's sister and her husband owned. He loved both of his jobs because he got to talk to just about everybody who came to town. Mr. Rudolf had lived in Crooked Creek all his long life, and he never left town except when one of the clubs he belonged to had a picnic at the nearby Beech Woods State Park. "Everything I need is here," he said, "so why should I go anywhere else?"

Mr. Rudolf owned the small house where Jenny and her mother had their second-floor apartment, and he lived downstairs. The house was green with white trim, and the gift shop where Jenny's mother worked was right across the street.

When Jenny reached the laundromat, she saw that Mr. Rudolf was talking with a couple of tourists, so she waited until they went into the Art Center. Then she gave him the refreshments Genevieve had sent. "Am I glad to see this iced tea!" he said, "I've been busy all day, and it sure is hot. They say all of the motels are full already, and the lodge at the Beech Woods is completely booked right through August."

Certainly Main Street was full of out-of-towners. The parking places by the laundromat were filled, and people were unloading their laundry from cars and vans crammed with suitcases, sleeping bags, and children.

"Jenny, you remember about my party tomorrow night, don't you?" Mr. Rudolf asked.

"Of course. I love parties, and I've never been to an eightieth birthday party before."

"To tell the truth," Mr. Rudolf said, "this is the first birthday party I've had since I was a boy. I don't know why I didn't do this sooner. I hope your mother can come. Or will she have to work at the gift shop?"

"I'm afraid she'll have to work."

"Well, I'll speak to the boss. Maybe I can arrange for her to get off early."

"I'm going to bring something special," Jenny said.

"Oh, don't bother about that. I just want you to be with me. It's the company that counts."

But Jenny had already planned a surprise for Mr. Rudolf, who was one of her favorite people.

"Do you have to go straight home?" Mr. Rudolf asked. "Or could I ask you to do something for me?"

"I don't have to be home till six," Jenny said.

"Could you stop by McCoy's then? I haven't seen

him to ask him to the party, and he doesn't have a phone. I'll write out a note, so if he isn't there, you can put it through the mail slot."

So Jenny went around the corner to McCoy's bookstore. The sign on the store said "McCoy—Books from Everywhere—*Only* Books." People who came to McCoy's and asked for a greeting card or a magazine were sent away in disgrace. But there were all kinds of old and new books, and McCoy had a lot of steady customers who came from out of town to buy books they couldn't get anywhere else.

McCoy was a small, thin man with a lot of curly red hair and a red beard. He lived in the rooms behind the store, and those were full of books, too. There were sturdy shelves in the store, but most of the books were in piles and in boxes and scattered around on tables and chairs. On the whole, McCoy didn't get around to arranging them on the shelves. He knew exactly where to find every book, though.

McCoy spent a lot of time reading in an easy chair by the front window, and he often seemed a little surprised when a customer came in. His hours were irregular because he liked to be outdoors a lot when the weather was good. Jenny saw that there was a card tacked on the bookstore door. It said, "Gone to the Beech Woods. May be open tomorrow." Jenny slipped Mr. Rudolf's note through the letter slot and went home.

(4)

When she got home, Ellery Aldrich was standing on his head in the living room, and Jenny's mother was timing him to see how long he could stay that way.

"Don't you feel a little dizzy?" Mrs. Reed asked, when he finally got on his feet again.

"More like hungry," Ellery said. "Do you happen to have a sandwich?"

"Would your mother mind?"

"How would she know?" Ellery asked.

"She might wonder why you aren't hungry at dinner time."

"She doesn't eat dinner when I do. Me and Hilary and the housekeeper eat together, and my mother and dad eat much, much later. Sometimes they don't eat at all. So she'll never know. So how about a little sandwich?"

"How about half a sandwich?" Jenny's mother said, and she went to the kitchen to fix one.

Jenny and Ellery followed.

"Mom, will you be able to get off work for Mr. Rudolf's party tomorrow night?"

"I doubt it. I'm going to try, though."

"What time is the party?" Ellery asked. "I need a celebration before I go to camp."

"Were you invited?" Jenny asked.

"I will be," Ellery said. "He and I are friends."

"He'll be invited," Jenny's mother said, handing him his sandwich. "Now take this with you, Ellery. Jenny and I are going to have supper now."

While they had supper, Jenny and Mrs. Reed talked some more about the party. Mrs. Reed had the next morning off, and she was scheduled to work in the evening. She decided that after supper she would walk over to the gift shop and ask Miss Golf if she could have time off to go to the party. "After all, he is eighty!" she said, "and I never ask for time off."

Greta Golf's Gift Shop where Mrs. Reed worked was full of beautiful things. There was a big sign on the front door that said:

> NO FOOD IN THE SHOP
> NO BARE FEET IN THE SHOP
> NO ANIMALS IN THE SHOP
> NO CHILDREN IN THE SHOP

Miss Golf had traveled to Indianapolis to have this sign specially made, because, she said, things were going to pieces in Crooked Creek.

It was always very quiet in the gift shop, and people tended to whisper. They bought a lot of things, too. Jenny's mother said that when Miss Golf looked at them with her pale, cold eyes, they were afraid to leave without buying.

Miss Golf always wore gray. She had gray dresses, gray blouses, gray skirts, and gray sweaters. They all matched her short, straight hair exactly. Although she was shaped like a large teddy bear, she wasn't cuddly and cheerful like a teddy bear. She was all business. She never said please, thank you, hello, or good-bye, because, in her opinion, these words were just time-wasters.

Coffee breaks were another time-waster, Miss Golf believed. She didn't leave her shop to go to

Genevieve's for coffee as almost every other business person in Crooked Creek did, and she didn't let Jenny's mother go, either. Occasionally, for special customers who bought a lot of things, she prepared spiced tea in her private office. Jenny's mother had to bring coffee or tea from home if she wanted any.

Jenny didn't dare go into the gift shop to see her mother except in emergencies, and she never seemed to have any emergencies. Sometimes she could see her mother inside, though, and sometimes her mother saw her and waved to her.

Mrs. Reed was very nervous about going over to ask Miss Golf for time off, and when she came back she said, "It doesn't look good, but maybe she'll change her mind."

Nothing is going to go right this summer, Jenny thought.

Late the next afternoon, Jenny looked around the kitchen gloomily. Every bowl and pan and spoon they owned had been used. There was flour on the counter and sugar on the floor, and there were all sorts of things to put away. But the saddest thing of all was the cake she had just baked for Mr. Rudolf's eightieth birthday.

She had wanted it to look beautiful like the ones in her mother's cookbook. Jenny had spent a long time choosing a recipe, and she had tried to follow it very carefully, but baking a fancy cake was much harder than she had imagined, even though she'd given up on the idea of putting the year of Mr. Rudolf's birth on top with frosting.

The project took a surprisingly long time, and the little kitchen got terribly hot, and when she was finished, instead of a beautiful birthday cake, she had a sprawling, hard object with an uneven top. She had trouble putting on the frosting, and it ended up in crumby globs. Jenny longed to get out of the kitchen and out of the apartment, but she wanted to get everything cleared away before her mother came home and saw the mess.

I should have talked to her about it, Jenny thought, and I should have let her help me with it. But Jenny had wanted to make this cake all by herself. Well, she had. And now look at it!

There was a hearty knock on the door. Jenny knew that it would be Mr. Rudolf because anyone else would ring the downstairs bell rather than knock on the door upstairs. Oh, no, she thought, but she went to the door.

"Hi," Mr. Rudolf said. "Would you like to come downstairs and help me set things up for the party?"

"Oh," Jenny said.

"Don't you want to?"

"Oh, yes, I want to," Jenny said, "but I can't come right now because I have to clean up the kitchen, and it's an awful mess."

"What happened to it?" Mr. Rudolf asked. "If the

sink got stopped up again, I'll take care of it before your mother gets home," and before Jenny could stop him, he marched to the kitchen like the good landlord he was. There on the table sat the cake. Mr. Rudolf looked at it and at all the pans and bowls and spoons.

"My," he said. "Did you do all this yourself?"

"I'm afraid so," Jenny said. "I wanted to make a really great birthday cake for you. But something went wrong, and it looks awful, and I'm very sorry."

"But I like it! What a good idea."

"I don't know what it will taste like," Jenny said.

"I'm not one bit worried about that. This is a great surprise! Thank you, Jenny.

"Now let's get the kitchen cleaned up, and then we can take the cake downstairs and put some candles on it. Greta Golf is coming early, and then she'll go back to the gift shop and send your mother over, so we'd better get going."

(6)

When Jenny arrived at the party, only Miss Golf was there, but some others soon came—Dave, Genevieve, McCoy, Ellery Aldrich, Dave's sister and her husband, and some of Mr. Rudolf's other friends who were about his age. Albert, Mr. Rudolf's big old cat, was there, too, lying on the mantel and looking very important.

The cake Jenny had baked was on a round table right in the middle of the living room. There were a great many red, white, and blue candles on it, and it didn't look too bad. There was a lot of other food, too. Everybody who came to the party brought some except McCoy, who brought books.

"So this is the cake Jenny baked," Genevieve said.

"She didn't use a mix, either," Mr. Rudolf said. "Not many people go to so much trouble these day."

"It's kind of collapsed, though," Jenny said. "Aren't they usually higher in the middle?"

"Sometimes they are, and sometimes they aren't," Dave said. "Some of the best cakes I've eaten have been—well—slanted like that one. It has distinction."

Dave was wearing a sweatshirt with "Coach Shapiro" written across the back. A lot of his clothes were unclaimed things from the laundromat Lost and Found. He was one of those rumpled people who always looked as if he had just been through a windstorm. He was well known as an Indiana artist, and once had had his picture in the Indianapolis Sunday paper. Jenny had hardly recognized him because he was wearing a coat and tie and his hair was under control. Just about all of her friends had cut out the picture and saved it. Even Miss Golf had it displayed in her office. "It can't hurt business," she said.

Every afternoon Dave worked in the big front window of the Art Center, but in his house he had another studio, where he did the painting and drawing he really cared about.

Dave and the others were enjoying themselves,

but Greta Golf was not in a party mood. "I wish you would do something about your mother," she said to Jenny.

Jenny didn't like this conversation, but Miss Golf went right on. "She doesn't organize her life right, that's the trouble. She doesn't eat right, doesn't get enough fresh air, doesn't think positively. She needs to pull herself together. I tell her all the time that she's doing everything wrong, but she doesn't change. See if you can get her on the right track."

Dave was standing nearby, and he said, "Greta, you're absolutely right." This interested everyone because Dave and Miss Golf had never been known to agree about anything before. "Of course Jenny's mother should get out and do more," he said. "For example, I'm sure she could get a much better job if she'd only try."

Miss Golf turned red and sputtered, "That's the biggest foolishness I've ever heard of. Why, there are fifty people in the county who'd give anything for Betty Reed's job. And what other job could she get, anyway? Just tell me that."

Mr. Rudolf interrupted them. "I know you're in a terrible hurry to get back to the shop, Greta," he said. "I'll cut the cake now so you can have some before you leave. Be sure to send Betty over right away."

Jenny and Ellery lighted the candles, and everyone sang "Happy Birthday" very loudly, except Miss Golf, who didn't seem to know the words. Dave took a piece of cake to her.

"You know perfectly well that I never touch sweets!" Miss Golf said. "Are you trying to kill me?"

"I'll eat it," Ellery said.

Miss Golf lowered her voice then, to say to Jenny, "I never should have come tonight. Unwholesome food, crowded rooms—all terrible for me. But then, I couldn't disappoint Willy Rudolf. After all, he's one of the few decent people left in town."

Then she got up from her chair and said loudly, "Well, happy birthday, Willy. I'll be getting back to work now. And by the way, this is for you." Out of her enormous handbag, she took a fat purple candle, which she gave to him, explaining that she hadn't been able to sell it in the shop even though she had marked it down twice.

"Thank you, Greta," Mr. Rudolf said. "It's nice you could celebrate with me."

Everyone felt much better when Miss Golf had gone.

"How's your summer going?" Dave asked Jenny.

"Okay," Jenny said, "but I sure wish there were more kids around."

"I'd like that myself," Dave said. "When I was growing up, there were lots of kids in those big houses up on the hill, and some down here, too. But now, most of the people with kids seem to live over in the new part of town. Have you heard from Mary Ellen?"

"Yes," Jenny said, "but it sure isn't the same as seeing her every day."

Then Dave saw Jenny's mother come in. "Here's your mom," he said.

"We were talking about you a while ago," Genevieve said to Mrs. Reed.

"What on earth could you find to say about

me?" Jenny's mother asked.

"We all think you could find a better job," Dave said. "All but G. Golf, that is. She just thinks you should work harder at the one you have!" Everyone but Jenny's mother laughed. She looked worried.

"I'm lucky to have any job at all," Mrs. Reed said.

"That's what Greta wants you to think," Genevieve said. "With all the building they're doing around here, there are going to be lots of new jobs. If you worked in an office, you wouldn't have to put up with Greta."

"Oh, Genevieve, I don't have the training for that."

"You could take some evening courses at the high school," Dave said.

"How would I get to the high school with no car?"

"I can probably find a ride for you," Genevieve said. "You think about it now."

"You'd better think fast," Ellery said. "How old are you, anyway?"

But Jenny's mother didn't seem to be interested.

Dave gave Mr. Rudolf a wonderful drawing of Albert which he had made for his birthday. "He's a great model," Dave said. "He can go for hours without moving a whisker." Mr. Rudolf put the drawing on the mantel, right beside the real Albert, who had turned his back and gone to sleep.

Everyone stayed for a long time. It was very late when Jenny went to sleep. Parties were so good. Her friends were so good. If only there were someone her age . . . .

(7)

The next morning, Jenny and her mother had a nice long breakfast together. Mrs. Reed had the morning off again and was going to work that evening. After breakfast, she walked to the laundromat. Jenny cleaned up the breakfast things and made the beds. After that, she sat down to work on a puzzle for a while. It was an enormous one that Mr. Rudolf had given her for her tenth birthday, and she would probably be seventeen before she got it all put together.

Jenny noticed that it was five to nine when she sat down. Much, much later she let herself look at the clock again, and it was nine eighteen. "Oh," she moaned, "oh, oh, oh, oh! This is the dumbest summer!" It seemed like months since the last day of school, and it had only been a week and a half. School isn't great, she thought, but at least there are kids around, and when you wake up in the morning, you know you'll be doing something. She stared at the hundreds of tiny puzzle pieces for a while, and then she made herself concentrate on putting it together.

About an hour later, the phone rang. "Hi, there, Jenny dear!" someone said. It was Mrs. Aldrich— Hilary and Ellery's mother. Every now and then Mrs. Aldrich called up. She always started out by saying, "Hi, there, Jenny dear," which Jenny hated.

"Hello, Mrs. Aldrich," Jenny said.

"How cute of you to recognize my voice!" said Mrs. Aldrich. "Jenny dear, Hilary has grown so much that a lot of her clothes are too small. Would you be very offended if we offered them to you? Someone ought to get some good out of them."

Jenny longed to say that she didn't want the clothes, but she knew her mother couldn't buy her much, and she really had to say yes. Lots of her clothes had originally been Hilary's. They were nice—it wasn't that—but there was something about the way Mrs. Aldrich spoke to her—and it was so tiresome to run into Hilary and have her say, "Oh, I remember when I got *that*."

Jenny said, "Sure, Mrs. Aldrich, I can use them."

"Just come by and pick them up then," Mrs. Aldrich said. "Mrs. Bartle will be here, of course, so come any time."

Mrs. Bartle was the only housekeeper in Crooked Creek. When the Aldrich family had moved there from Indianapolis, Mrs. Bartle came with them, and she made no secret of the fact that she didn't like the town.

"If they didn't need me so much," Mrs. Bartle told Genevieve, "I'd go right back to the city in a minute."

"They need her, all right," Genevieve said. "That Mrs. Aldrich couldn't butter a piece of toast. And Mrs. Bartle told me that sometimes she wears her bathrobe all day—never does get dressed!"

Jenny thought that it would be nice to wear a bathrobe all day now and then, especially the kind of beautiful bathrobe Mrs. Aldrich owned. She did have to admit, though, that Ellery's mother was a most unpleasant woman. It was strange that for all her smiles and greetings, she left you with the feeling that you were just like one of the weeds that grew out of the cracks in the sidewalk.

When Jenny's mother came home from her errands, Jenny told her about Mrs. Aldrich's call.

"She came into the gift shop yesterday," Mrs. Reed said. "She bought fifty-eight dollars' worth of candles."

"Wow," said Jenny.

"I guess you need the clothes," Mrs. Reed said, "but I wish we could get you new things, instead."

"Me, too," Jenny said. Then she wished she hadn't said that, because she knew they didn't have much money to spend. "Hilary's things will be fine," she said. "I don't need anything else."

"I should learn to sew," her mother said. "I should learn to do so many things." She got a look on her face that Jenny hated.

"I'll be learning to sew soon," Jenny said. "Then I can make something for both of us."

Her mother didn't seem to hear. "I've got to go to work," she said, taking her lunch dishes to the sink.

That afternoon, Jenny decided to go to Genevieve's for a while. When she finished there, she could go by Hilary and Ellery's house and pick up the clothes if she felt like it.

Genevieve's was nearly full when she got there, and there was plenty for her to do. It was good to be busy and to be around people. After a while the crowd thinned out, and then Ellery came in, carrying a bag from the new Yumburger place.

"Don't bring that stuff in here!" Genevieve said crossly. "Yumburgers! Frozen stuff!"

"The bag is empty," Ellery said. "I just had an order of fries is all. Toss it in the trash for me, will you?" He sat down at the counter and reached for the menu.

Ellery's hair stood straight up on top of his head, his shirt was buttoned crooked, his shorts were ripped, and his sneakers were untied. He was also very dirty.

"I'll have a cinnamon doughnut and a grilled cheese sandwich and some grape Sparkle," he said, after he had looked at the menu for a long time.

"Terrible!" said Genevieve. "Terrible, terrible!"

But she got Ellery what he asked for. "I suppose this is your lunch," she said.

"Well, of course not. I always eat lunch at home. But today we only had soup and oranges. I need more than that. Especially since Hilary and I are going to camp tomorrow, which means nothing to eat for the rest of the summer."

"Are you going tomorrow?" Jenny asked. "I didn't know it was that soon." She hated the thought of Ellery going away. He wasn't perfect, but he was someone to talk to.

"We leave right after breakfast."

"It must be fun."

"Oh, Jenny, you're so wrong. You can't believe how dumb it is. They wake you up at seven in the morning with a bell. Can you believe that? You have to make your bed and sweep the cabin! You have to take showers! And for snacks they have stuff like dried prunes! You'd better give me another doughnut."

Ellery didn't know, of course, how much Jenny would have liked to go to camp.

"Jenny . . ." Ellery said.

"Yes."

"Come on over to the house today. I'm going to let you in on something."

"Oh, I don't know . . . ." Jenny had learned to be cautious with Ellery. He loved to take chances, and he also loved to play jokes.

"Believe me, Jenny, this is something really special. You'll never guess what it is."

"I might be over. I'll see."

When Ellery left, Genevieve fished some coins from under his plate. Ellery was the only one of the Crooked Creek regulars who tipped. She dropped the money in the collection box by the cash register.

(8)

Later on, when Jenny left Genevieve's, she remembered the clothes Mrs. Aldrich had asked her to pick up. She might as well go to Hilary and Ellery's now. She wandered back up Main Street, and at the corner by Tree House Antiques, she started up the hill to their house.

This was Jenny's favorite part of town. Once, more than a hundred years before, the courthouse at the very top of the hill and the houses around it had been all there was of Crooked Creek.

The houses on the hill were old and large, and each was very different from the others. They had towers and porches and balconies and huge garages that had once been barns. Jenny thought they were wonderful. Most of them sat on big green lawns. The principal of Jenny's school lived in one of them; she saw him hammering at a railing and waved. Miss Golf owned a big dark gray one and rented one floor of it to an old cousin who was even crankier than Miss Golf herself. It was beautiful on the hill, but not many children lived there. Except for some very small ones, there were only Hilary and Ellery.

Jenny opened the Aldriches' gate, went up the walk, and rang the bell. She knew that it would be quite a while before anyone came to the door. Mrs. Bartle, the housekeeper, had bad feet and didn't move very fast, and nobody else ever answered the door. After a while, Mrs. Bartle opened it and looked at Jenny blankly, although Jenny had been there many times before.

"I'm Jenny," said Jenny patiently. "Mrs. Aldrich asked me to come by to get a package."

"Oh," Mrs. Bartle said. "Hilary's old clothes." She walked to a corner of the entrance hall and got a big shopping bag, which she handed to Jenny.

"Is Ellery here?" Jenny asked.

Mrs. Bartle sighed, as if this question were the very one that would put an end to her. "He's in the basement," she said. "I guess it would be all right if you go on down."

The Aldriches' basement was quite a bit larger than Jenny's whole apartment. Among other things, it had a full kitchen, and Ellery was in this kitchen now, spreading crackers with peanut butter.

"How can you be hungry again so soon? And I thought you weren't allowed to cook."

"It has nothing to do with being hungry," Ellery said, "and I'm only not allowed to cook upstairs—not that this is cooking. Okay, let's go."

"To where?"

"To where the thing I want to show you is."

"Aren't you going to put the lid on the peanut butter?"

"You know, you're going to be Mrs. Bartle when you grow up," Ellery said. "I'll take care of that later. Come on."

Jenny followed Ellery upstairs and out the back door. They pushed through the lilac hedge and went down Mr. Fitzgerald's driveway. Then they crossed the street and went down Judge Gitlin's driveway and crawled under his hedge. They were in the backyard of a house that Jenny had always admired. It was painted yellow with lots of white trim, and it was tall and spreading, with many windows. The front porch went part way around one side, too, and there was a big sleeping porch on the second floor. Mr. and Mrs. Morton, who were very old, had lived there for years and years, but now they lived at the Methodist Home, and the house had been empty for several months. There was an Englebart's Estates sign on the front lawn to show that it was for sale.

"Come on," Ellery said, and he went around to the side. Here, too, there was a tall, thick hedge which made the yard very private. Ellery walked over to one of the basement windows and gave it a push. It was hinged at the top, and it swung in. "Look," he said, "we can get in."

"Are you kidding?" Jenny said. "We'd get in all kinds of trouble!"

"Come on."

"Ellery, there's a *judge* living right over there!"

But Ellery was sliding through the window. He

dropped to the basement floor, picked himself up, and grinned at her. Before she knew it, Jenny had handed him the bag of clothes and followed him in. It was exciting—fun!

It was even more fun to go upstairs and see the rest of the house. They ran through it, looking in every room and opening every cupboard and closet. There was plenty of room to turn handsprings. It was a fast, smooth ride down the banister. They shouted through the clothes chute, and they laughed and laughed.

"Maybe there's a treasure here!" Ellery said. "A hidden safe with a million dollars in it, or rare coins, or a letter written by Abraham Lincoln." They didn't find any of those things, although they searched very carefully. But there was a colored window shaped like a star, a tiny room with nothing in it but a huge, old-fashioned bathtub, and book-shelves in every room—even the kitchen.

"Maybe we could start a resort here," Ellery said. "I could be the manager, and you could be the recreation director and plan all the parties and games and activities."

"Hilary would want to be the manager," Jenny said, "and she'd make you be the janitor." Ellery nodded sadly.

"I wonder what time it is," Jenny said. "I'll bet it's almost suppertime. I'd better get home. Mom will be there."

"We have to go out the side door," Ellery said, "because we can lock it from the inside." He pushed a button on the inside knob and closed the door carefully and quietly after them. "It's locked," he whispered. "See you." And Jenny hurried home.

(9)

When Jenny got home, she found that it was much later than she had thought. Her mother had been home for her supper break and had gone back to the gift shop. There was a note in the middle of the kitchen table which said, "Where are you, Jenny Reed? You had better have a good answer!"

Then there was a knock on the door. It was Mr. Rudolf.

"Now, where did you disappear to?" he asked. "Your mom turned the town upside down looking for you and missed her supper."

"I was playing with Ellery."

"But we looked there. Your mother called the Aldriches' and Genevieve and everybody we could think of."

"Well—see—we were just wandering around. We didn't know it was so late. We were wandering around up on the hill." Jenny felt miserable. How stupid to lie to Mr. Rudolf, one of her best friends.

"You'd better call your mother at work," he said. "She was worried."

Jenny forced herself to call the gift shop, praying Miss Golf wouldn't answer. Mrs. Reed answered, and Jenny tried to explain where she had been, without really *saying* where she had been. It was not a good explanation. Jenny could imagine what her mother would have said if she had been at home, but because she was at work, her mother couldn't talk much. Maybe she wouldn't be so angry by the time she got home. When she worked nights, she usually went right to bed.

What fun the afternoon had been, though. It was the most wonderful house. Now she would have it to remember. Of course, she would never go there again.

(10)

Jenny woke up very early the next morning. She felt uneasy and tired, too. She wanted to go back to sleep, but she knew she couldn't. There was something she had forgotten, something she was supposed to do—the clothes! She had left Hilary's clothes in the house. They were still in the basement! Oh, no! What should she do? Maybe Ellery would get them for her—no, Ellery was going to camp first thing that day.

Should she go back for them? Jenny didn't want to—she was terrified at the thought—but she couldn't leave them there. Mrs. Aldrich might mention them to her mother on one of her many trips to the gift shop. She would just have to go back. She would pick up the clothes and run.

As soon as her mother left for work, Jenny went back to the house. She felt like a criminal as she opened the basement window. But as long as she was there, she couldn't resist looking at it again, all of it. She kept the bag of clothes with her so she wouldn't forget it again.

When she had worked her way up to the farthest corner of the third floor, Jenny walked slowly down the stairs and into the living room. The sun shone warmly on one particular spot, and Jenny sat down in it. Then she said out loud, "This is my home, and I love it."

She surprised herself by saying it. Her home was on Main Street, and she knew it, and she liked it there. But this house was so warm, so comforting, so friendly. She felt different here. She closed her eyes and rested in the sun.

(11)

Jenny didn't stop going to the house. In fact, she went there almost every day. It became her best friend. It had nothing to do but listen to her, and it didn't mind at all when she filled it full of imaginary relatives and friends and furniture and parties.

Now when she walked past the stores, she looked in the windows and thought, That wicker chair would be just right for the porch, and that quilt would be perfect for my bedroom.

How nice it would be to have meals in the cheerful breakfast room or in the dining room with its small fireplace.

Her own mother would be there, of course, but in this house, Jenny's mother would smile a lot and invite people over. And to keep her company, there would be a father with a strong, deep voice. He'd be with us in the evenings, Jenny thought. He'd fix things and talk to us, and we could take walks and play ball and get a badminton set . . . .

There would be other people in the family, too. Of course, there would be Linda. How pleased she'd be to have her own room, so that when she came home from college, she didn't have to sleep on the couch right in the middle of things. A twin sister would be nice, too. They could be in the same class at school, and when school was out, her sister would still be there to keep her company. Jenny thought she would like at least one brother, and in such a big house she could have a dog—no, two dogs, one big and one little. And a cat like Albert, but Jenny's cat would have kittens a lot, which Albert never did, of course.

It was thoughts like this that kept Jenny busy when she went to the house—and when she was away from it, too. She knew, though she tried not to think about it, that she shouldn't be going there. But it was so good to have a special place of her own.

(12)

Late in June a letter came for Jenny's mother.
Jenny thought that the chunky writing was her
father's. She studied the envelope, turned it over,
and laid it on the kitchen table.

When Mrs. Reed came home from work, she saw
the letter, but she didn't pick it up. It stayed there
on the table while they had supper, and neither
mentioned it. When Jenny went to bed that night,
the letter was still unopened, but the next morning
when she got up, it was gone. Her mother had left
for work. Jenny did the jobs she had been asked to
do, and then she went over to the house. She didn't
do much there, just walked through it and told it
about the letter.

When she went home for lunch, she found her
mother making sandwiches.

"Your dad has invited you to come and visit him,"
she said, not looking at Jenny.

Jenny's heart jumped. "You mean, he wants me

to come to Indianapolis?"

"Yes. I'm not sure if we can work it out. I have to think about it some more. It's a long way. And you're young. And . . . ." Her voice trailed off. "Anyway, I'll think about it. You think about it, too."

Jenny couldn't seem to think about it. She could only feel about it. She felt something like the time when a kid handcuffed her to his swing set and then forgot her and went fishing, and something like the time when she had to recite a poem at a PTA meeting, and something like the time when Mary Ellen and her family drove out of town for good.

Jenny didn't really remember her father very well. His name was Joe. Some years he sent a Christmas card or some birthday money, and she had a snapshot of him that she had found long ago in a waste basket, but that was really all that she knew of him except for hazy memories.

She didn't want to hear from him now because it made her wonder why he didn't act like a father. What was wrong with her, or with him, or with her mother, that made him stay away? What was the point of his asking her to come and see him now?

Just a few days ago, she had envied the kids who were going away to camp or on vacation. Now, she felt that leaving town would be the worst thing in the world. What if she didn't like her father? That would be terrible, but if she did like him and then she didn't get to see him again . . . .

Maybe I should wait till I'm older, Jenny thought. Yes, she would wait. She felt relieved. After her mother went back to work, Jenny ran down to Genevieve's, putting the letter and Joe Reed out of her mind.

What a shock it was when her mother came into Genevieve's in the middle of the afternoon.

"I can't believe it!" said Genevieve. "How did you ever get away?"

"Give me some iced tea, will you?" Jenny's mother asked, sitting down at the counter. "I have exactly four minutes to sit here." Then she said to Genevieve, "Joe wants Jenny to visit him."

"Oh."

"He wants her to come for a week at the end of July."

Genevieve said nothing.

"I've decided to wait till I'm older," Jenny said. No one paid any attention.

"She couldn't travel alone," Mrs. Reed said. "She's only ten. I wouldn't want her to travel alone. She gets carsick, you know."

"And buses are worse!" Jenny said. "I'd probably be taking the bus, and people who get carsick usually get *much sicker* on buses!"

Jenny's mother said, "I'm going to tell him she can't come. Not now."

"It isn't a long ride," Genevieve said. "I know it seems a million miles away, but it takes less than three hours on the bus. It would make a change for her."

"That awful town!" Mrs. Reed said.

"I'll be going up to my sister's some time in July," Genevieve said. "Of course I don't usually leave the restaurant, but I've got to have some work done on my teeth up there. Jenny and I could take the bus up together, or maybe I can find us a ride."

Jenny's mother swirled her iced tea around in the glass.

"Only if you want her to go, of course, Betty," Genevieve said.

"I'll have to think about it some more." Abruptly Mrs. Reed left.

"She forgot to pay," Jenny said. "She never does that."

"Never mind."

Jenny felt turned upside down again. She isn't going to let me have anything to say about whether or not I go, she thought bitterly. She started to bang some silverware onto a tray.

"Don't worry yourself about it," Genevieve said. "It will work out."

"Nothing ever works out!" Jenny said.

(13)

"If you want to go, you can," Jenny's mother said on Saturday morning.

Jenny was startled. Nothing more had been said about her going to Indianapolis, and she had almost convinced herself that the issue was closed.

"He says he'll send your ticket. It *is* a chance for you to go somewhere, and heaven knows you don't have many of them. I really think you ought to go . . . ." But Jenny had a feeling that her mother didn't mean that.

"Maybe when I'm older?" she asked.

"It isn't going to get any easier," her mother said. "That's the one thing on earth I'm sure of."

Later, Jenny went to Genevieve's Restaurant. Dave was at the counter with Sam Englebart of Englebart's Estates. They were talking to Genevieve about the house—Jenny's house on the hill!

"I've only showed it twice in all this time," Mr. Englebart said. "Now, if it was on the north end of town, and half the size, I could sell it in a day."

"That place will never sell," Genevieve said.

"Oh, I hope not!" Jenny said.

"What makes you say a thing like that?" Genevieve asked. "What do you care about it?"

"Oh, I don't know," Jenny mumbled. She would have to be more careful.

Genevieve said, "Now if I get a house—not that I need one—I'd want it all on one floor, with a utility room and an attached garage."

"Not me," Jenny said. Then she fidgeted around while Genevieve and Dave and Sam Englebart talked about the new shopping center that was about to open on the north edge of town. Finally they left, and Genevieve noticed Jenny scowling at her.

"You got something on your mind?" she asked.

"Genevieve, I don't know if I should go or not."

"To see your dad? That's not for me to say."

"I don't think Mom wants me to go," Jenny said, "but I'm not sure. I can't tell from what she says."

"She doesn't know herself," Genevieve said. "It's a mixed-up business."

"Why did they split up, Genevieve?"

"Oh, honey, I don't know."

"Genevieve, you do!"

"Listen, honey," Genevieve said, "I know I talk a lot, but I don't like to talk about other people's problems. Someday, when she's ready, your mom will tell you about it herself."

"Okay," Jenny said reluctantly. Genevieve was usually right about people. She would just have to wait. But there was another thing.

"Genevieve, why did Mom go to the hospital that time when I was little?"

"Oh, that was a long time ago."

"But why did she go?"

"She was very, very unhappy."

"People don't go to the hospital because they're unhappy!"

"Sometimes they do. Your mom was unhappy all the time. She couldn't take care of you girls. She was tired out and worried and sad after your dad went away—and even before he went away. Your dad was—is—a good man, but it's hard for him to stick to things. He always did have that problem.

He loved all of you, but he wasn't really up to the responsibility. He was always getting distracted. Anyway, your mom was worn out. She went to the hospital for a while, and now she's okay. The hospital bills were something awful, of course, and that was another thing for her to deal with."

"Is that why Miss Golf acts like she's doing us a favor to let Mom work for her?"

"I don't think so. Greta's always been a pain, since we were girls. I wish your mom would try for another job. I know she could get one, but she's afraid to take the chance."

"Anyway," Jenny said, "I don't know what to do about Indianapolis."

"It wouldn't be right for me to interfere," Genevieve said. "It *would* be good for you to see another part of the world. But it's for you and your mom to work out.

"I will say this much, though," Genevieve added, after a few minutes.

"Yes?"

"I think you ought to go."

(14)

It wasn't the answer Jenny wanted. She went to the house on the hill to think it over. Inside, she huddled on the floor in one of the second-floor bedrooms. Why wasn't this house her home? Why wasn't her mother in the yard, talking with a neighbor and smiling? Why wasn't her father trimming the shrubbery or cutting the grass? Jenny got up and trailed through the house. It wasn't right for such a house to sit empty. It should be hers. Hers, her mother's, her father's, her sisters' and brothers', her dogs' . . . and she was off again, making the house her own and her imaginary family's.

It all had to end after a while, and she went back to the hot, empty little apartment.

(15)

There was hardly anyone in Genevieve's Restaurant the next afternoon.

"Where is everyone?" Jenny asked.

Then Genevieve reminded her of the grand opening at the new shopping center. Everyone was there. Genevieve was down in the dumps.

"Come on, now!" said Sam Englebart, who was sitting at the counter. "They'll be back. Why, what are they going to find out there to compare with your good cooking and baking?"

"Oh, I know mine is better," Genevieve said, "but when I think how much work it is to keep going here, I do wonder . . . ."

A customer came in.

"Oh, this just tops it off!!" Genevieve muttered.

It was Mrs. Bartle. It was her day off, and she looked different from her everyday self. When she was working, she wore a white dress like a nurse's uniform and very large, flat white shoes. She didn't wear jewelry on working days, and she didn't wear much makeup, either. Today, though, she had put on a lot of pink makeup and a little bit of red makeup, and she had made a dark line above her eyebrows which gave her a surprised look. She was wearing large white earrings and large white beads and a large white pin shaped like a flower. She carried a shiny white pocketbook.

Most people who came into Genevieve's Restaurant alone sat at the counter, but Mrs. Bartle went to a booth with four places set, and she sat down between two of the places and put her pocketbook on the table. Then she folded her hands and stared straight ahead of her.

"Afternoon," Genevieve said, going over to see what she wanted. Jenny poured a glass of water and came along.

It took Mrs. Bartle a very long time to order. It wasn't a simple matter. She had to know just how everything was cooked, and she had to consider what she had had for breakfast and what she was going to have for dinner. At last, Mrs. Bartle was served ham and green beans and mashed potatoes and a roll and apple butter and iced tea. Then she wanted Genevieve to sit down with her.

"I shouldn't," Genevieve said, but she sat down. "I'm not exactly overworked today," she said. Jenny sat down, too, although she hadn't been asked to.

"You can't think how glad I am of my day off!" said Mrs. Bartle, starting to cut up the ham into tiny, delicate pieces.

"You pretty busy?" Genevieve asked.

"Oh!" said Mrs. Bartle. "They can't do a thing for themselves, you know, not a thing! Those folks depend on me for everything. And the size of that place! It's something to keep up, I'll tell you. And, of course, them and their parties. Now that the children are at camp, they'll really get going with their parties! They'll have all kinds of people coming in from Indianapolis. I could tell you things . . . ."

Jenny waited hopefully, but Mrs. Bartle glanced at her and then said to Genevieve, "Some other time."

"Did you know, Mrs. Bartle," said Genevieve, "that Jenny's going to Indianapolis for a visit?"

Jenny wished that Genevieve hadn't mentioned it, but for the first time, Mrs. Bartle looked at Jenny and really seemed to see her. "Oh, you lucky little thing!" she said. "That's a lovely city! The homes! The stores! The governor's mansion!" She was quiet for a little while, chewing away on her ham and seeming to concentrate with enormous pleasure on the good living that was going on in Indianapolis.

"I don't see what's so wonderful about it," Genevieve said. "My sister lives there, and it seems to me like a big ugly place. And so flat . . . ."

"Well, dear," Mrs. Bartle said, "it's the way they dress, the way they talk. Why, they're all like the Aldriches there."

Jenny and Genevieve sat thinking what a terrible place Indianapolis must be if it were full of people like the Aldriches.

"There's the Speedway, you know," Mrs. Bartle continued. "Where they have the big auto races.

And John Dillinger, the former Public Enemy Number One, is buried there. You can see his grave."

"Oh," Jenny said.

"Of course, you can get a very rough element there, too. Where my people lived, though, we didn't have much trouble."

"You mean where your family lived?" Jenny asked.

"No, my people that I helped out."

"You mean, your job?"

"That's right. They were wonderful people, and they always said they couldn't get along without me."

"Then why aren't you still there?"

Mrs. Bartle didn't answer right away. "They moved, you see," she said finally. "Into a smaller place. They didn't need much help anymore. So I went to the Aldriches'. And when they moved here, I came along. It's been a year now. To tell the truth," she said slowly, "I feel rather lonely here." She looked at Jenny. "I don't suppose a youngster like you would understand that, though."

"Oh, I do!" Jenny said. "Ever since my friend Mary Ellen moved away, I've felt lonely myself. It's an awful feeling." *

"Maybe your visit to Indianapolis will brighten up your summer," Mrs. Bartle said. Then she neatly folded her paper napkin and put her knife and fork together in the middle of her plate.

"I don't suppose I should have pie," she said. "No, I think I will have my pie later. After I've done my errands."

"When is your day off over?" Jenny asked.

"Oh, I don't do a thing for them until tomorrow," Mrs. Bartle said.

"How will you spend the rest of the day then?" Jenny asked, trying to imagine what a person like Mrs. Bartle would do to have fun.

"Why, I have all my errands!" Mrs. Bartle said. "And then, of course, I have lots of things to tend to at home. Like ironing my dresses and writing to my sister in California and—little chores, you know. Keeping things nice."

"You do keep your things very nice," Jenny said. "That's a pretty dress."

"Thank you, dear." The rest of Mrs. Bartle's face turned almost as red as the round spots of color on her cheeks, and she actually smiled at Jenny. "Well, I must hurry if I'm going to get everything done. Nice talking to you girls. Thank you so much, Miss Genevieve, and perhaps I'll stop in later for a little break." Mrs. Bartle picked up her pocketbook, paid her check, and went toward the door.

"I have gooseberry pie today, Ivy," Genevieve said. "So try to stop in later, and I'll put a piece by for you."

"That's sweet of you, dear," Mrs. Bartle said. "And if I have the time, I surely will."

Sometimes Jenny remembered things. She remembered the sound of her mother crying and crying. She remembered Linda shouting and slamming doors. She remembered Mary Ellen's father lifting her out of her crib, carrying her to Mary Ellen's house, and putting her on his wife's lap. She didn't know when those things had happened. No one talked of them. Maybe she had dreamed them.

(17)

One day when Jenny went over to talk to Mr. Rudolf, he was busy with something in front of the laundromat. At first she thought that he was drawing a picture, but then she saw that he was making a sign. It was like the signs in the yards of the big houses on the north end of town, except that the letters were a little shaky. KEEP OUT, it said. NO TRESPASSING.

"I hate to do this," Mr. Rudolf said, when Jenny looked at his sign. "I just hate it. But people are tearing up our yard. Pulling the vines off the fence and snapping off the tomato plants. I can't let it happen. But I don't like a sign like this." Mr. Rudolf stared at it sadly. Then at the bottom he added the word SORRY.

"That's better," he said. "It had to be done. Now, how are things going for you today?"

"Did you know I may go to Indianapolis?"

"I believe someone did mention that. Are you

going to visit your dad?"

"He's invited me. I'm not sure if I'm going. I don't think I want to go, and I don't think Mom wants me to go, but even so, I may go."

"You could use a little journey. After all, Indianapolis is the capital of Indiana. Everyone should see Indianapolis."

"Have you seen it?"

"Of course. As you know, I don't ordinarily leave Crooked Creek—I don't feel the need—but when I went into the army in World War I, I reported at the fort in Indianapolis. It' a very fine town. And a young person like you ought to see the state capital. Young people these days go to all sorts of places—Indianapolis, Cincinnati, Louisville . . . ."

"I haven't seen my father for so long," Jenny said. "I don't really remember him. He's married, and I don't know his wife. What would we talk about?"

"I haven't the least idea," Mr. Rudolf said. "But it could be a very good thing for you to go. And don't forget to climb the Soldiers and Sailors Monument. It's right in the middle of the city and very, very tall,

65

and if you climb it, you get a fine view. If I were to go back to Indianapolis, that's what I'd do."

"Mrs. Bartle said I should see the grave of John Dillinger, who used to be Public Enemy Number One," Jenny said.

Mr. Rudolf nodded. "Yes, he was an Indiana boy," he said. "If you do go to Indianapolis, remember me to your dad."

"It seems funny . . ." Jenny said. "It seems as if everyone in town knows my dad except me."

"I wouldn't call that funny myself," Mr. Rudolf said. "But then, I'm old and peculiar."

Jenny left then because a customer in the laundromat needed Mr. Rudolf's help. She sighed as she walked away. She wanted to forget all about Indianapolis and stay with her friends. They weren't kids, but at least she knew them and liked them. And she always had the house.

(18)

The trip to Indianapolis was set for the twentieth of July. A long way off.

Jenny tried not to think about it. She thought about the big house instead and visited it often while her mother was at work. She knew the house so well now that she could almost recognize a new speck of dust. She knew which of the steps squeaked and that the third floor got very, very hot in the afternoon. She didn't dare open a window to cool it off; still, the third floor was by far her favorite place. There were three little rooms there, and a hall lined with tall cupboards. The ceilings were slanted, and the windows were odd shaped. The wallpaper was old and faded and soothing. It didn't matter to Jenny that it was peeling off the walls.

One day Jenny was in her favorite room on the third floor wishing that Mary Ellen were there with her, helping her plan for the house and admiring it with her. Suddenly she felt that she had to get near some people. She ran downstairs, quietly let herself out the side door, and hurried over to Main Street.

Here there were plenty of people. The hot Indiana sun beat down on the townspeople and tourists who filled the sidewalks. A whole Boy Scout troop was climbing off a bus and heading for the laundromat with their backpacks. Mr. Rudolf would have his hands full. And another busload of very old people all dressed up in their good clothes had stopped near the Indiana Inn.

Genevieve's would be filled with people wanting cold drinks and ice cream, and Jenny decided to go there. Then, near the laundromat, she saw Susan, one of the farm kids from school, with her mother, and she went over to talk to them. Their washing machine had broken down, and they had brought their laundry to town, but the Boy Scouts had beaten them to the laundromat. Susan's mother decided to do some errands while Susan spent some time with Jenny. They went over to Jenny's apartment and had a good afternoon.

"You come out to the farm some day," Susan's

mother said, when she came to take Susan home. "I'll come and get you."

Jenny hoped they'd remember. It made such a difference when you could share things with a friend.

(19)

Jenny wondered what her father would think of her. She knew that she was ordinary-looking. She wished that there were something special about her, but there wasn't. She had plain brown hair, plain brown eyes, plain freckles, plain clothes. She bored herself. Hilary said that Jenny could easily be fixed up to look better, and she wanted to try it with some of Mrs. Aldrich's makeup and hair stuff, but Jenny didn't think it was any use.

Ellery said it didn't matter that she was boring-looking because he liked her, but that didn't make her feel any better. If this was a soap opera, she thought, or one of the romantic old stories that Mr. Rudolf had downstairs in his bookcase, her father would be rich and handsome, and she would be beautiful and popular, and they would be so thrilled with each other that they would never part. Jenny knew perfectly well that it wouldn't be that way. But what *would* it be like?

(20)

The day Jenny was to leave for Indianapolis, her mother took the day off from work, and there was an argument with Miss Golf.

"Why did you take the whole day off, anyway?" Jenny asked. "I don't leave till four o'clock, and all I have to do is walk down to Genevieve's just like I do every day."

"We have so much to do!" her mother said. They packed and unpacked Jenny's suitcase, always with the same things. Mrs. Reed ironed everything, even though she never ironed ordinarily. She checked all the buttons on Jenny's clothes to see if they were about to come off, and she sent Jenny to the drugstore for a new comb and toothbrush. Jenny hated the whole business.

When Jenny got back from the drugstore, her mother said, "You have to wear a dress."

"That's ridiculous!" Jenny said. "I won't be comfortable."

"I want you to look right!" Jenny's mother said

stubbornly. "I'm going to get your dress out of the suitcase," she said to Jenny, and she went into the bedroom. Something about the look on her mother's face made Jenny put on the dress without arguing any more. It was too short and cut into her shoulders, and she felt silly. Too bad there hadn't been a dress among the things Hilary had grown out of.

Mrs. Reed walked with Jenny to Genevieve's. They found Genevieve giving desperate, last-minute instructions to the twins, who were sprawled comfortably at a table as if they were the ones who were going on vacation.

"*No problem,*" was their response to everything Genevieve said to them, but she clearly didn't believe them.

"How will they ever manage?" Genevieve moaned. At least her misery got Mrs. Reed's attention away from Jenny for a while. Jenny sat staring out the big front window. She felt queasy, as if she were getting the flu. She was the first one to see the Indianapolis bus coming down Main Street. Unfortunately, the others soon saw it, too.

It was the longest ride in the world. Genevieve passed the time by naming all the things she was sure the twins would do wrong. Jenny got sick.

Doris, Genevieve's sister, jumped at them the moment they got off the bus in Indianapolis. She was a larger, pinker, louder version of Genevieve, and she was very anxious to get her sister onto another bus, which would take them to the faraway suburb where she lived.

"We'll go as soon as we find Jenny's dad," Genevieve said, setting down the two big shopping bags she had kept with her on the bus and searching for the claim checks for the suitcases. "He should be here." But there was no one waiting beside the bus or in the waiting room who could possibly be Joe Reed.

"Genevieve, we only have ten minutes till our bus leaves!" Doris said anxiously. "We probably won't get a seat now, and if we miss it, we'll have to stay downtown another two hours."

"We won't miss it!" said Genevieve. How tired Jenny was, and how she wished this were all over. "I'll call Joe's place," Genevieve said. "I have his number. If this isn't just like . . . ." She went to the pay phone, but she got no answer when she dialed.

"They must be on their way," Doris said. "The little girl will be all right till they get here. It's six o'clock. There's a lot of traffic at this hour, and he probably got caught in it. She'll be all right, and we'll call her dad's place as soon as we get home to make sure she got there. Come on now, Genevieve!"

Genevieve looked around the station one more time. Then she opened her purse. "Now, take this," she said, giving Jenny two dollars, "and go over to that counter and get yourself something to eat."

"Genevieve, I just threw up a little while ago," Jenny said wearily, but Genevieve paid no attention.

"See that policeman over there?" Genevieve went on. "Don't hesitate to go right over to him if you need any help. Or scream bloody murder if you need to. I don't like the looks of these people around here at all." Jenny looked at her in amazement.

"Genevieve, you're talking foolish!" Doris said, "and we're going to miss the bus."

"Have a nice time," Jenny said weakly, as Genevieve was dragged away. In Crooked Creek, Genevieve was queen. She knew all about everything. Here, though, she seemed timid and helpless as she followed Doris off to the other bus. And Jenny was feeling timid and helpless, too.

(22)

The bus station seemed to be fairly new, but apparently it had never been cleaned. Something about it made everyone look worn out and alarmed, and it smelled bad. Why had she come to this awful place? What if her father had forgotten she was coming?

I knew he wouldn't be here, I just knew it, she said to herself. She tried to tell herself that there was a good reason why there was no one there to meet her, but no reason could be good enough, no reason at all. She dragged herself over to an empty plastic chair and put her suitcase in front of her feet.

Across from her, a young woman slapped her baby who was sitting in a stroller, and he began to scream. Jenny wanted to scream, too. "I'll hold it," she said to the baby's mother without thinking. "I'll hold the baby," she repeated, as the mother stared at her.

"You want to?"

"Sure."

The mother, who was very young and had her hair in rollers, looked Jenny over.

"Okay, then, I'll make a phone call if you'll just watch him for a minute. You don't have to hold him, just watch him."

But Jenny took the fat, grimy baby out of his stroller and put him over her shoulder. He stopped crying at once and began to pull at her hair as if they were old friends. Jenny held him close and felt much safer. His mother, at the pay phone nearby, never took her eyes off them, but she kept on talking and talking. Jenny was glad. She wanted to go on holding the baby.

Then she saw a man and woman hurry through the main entrance. She was quite sure that the man was her father—she didn't know why she was sure. He was rather short, with dark hair. Jenny looked at the woman—at the gleaming white high-heeled shoes, the white dress, the perfectly molded bright yellow curls piled on top of her head. She's so *new!*

Jenny thought in amazement. This was her father's wife, Laura.

Suddenly the bus station seemed a fine, safe place. She wanted to stay there. For a crazy moment, she thought maybe they wouldn't see her, and she could get on another bus and go back home to her beautiful Crooked Creek. She'd gotten along without knowing her father so far, so why start now? The baby's mother pulled him away then and said, "Okay, thanks." Jenny stood up slowly, picked up her suitcase, and walked toward the man and woman.

It was a long drive to her father's place, and nobody said much. Jenny was praying she wouldn't throw up again. At last they came to a part of town where there were a lot of small brick apartment buildings with grass and shrubbery around them. There was nothing like them in Crooked Creek, and Jenny thought they were very pretty.

They parked behind one of them, and walked up two floors to her father's apartment. It was cool, and there was a purple carpet and nice-looking furniture. "This is beautiful!" Jenny said. The kitchen was tiny, but it had a yellow refrigerator and stove and a dishwasher. "What a nice place," Jenny said.

Almost immediately the phone rang, and Jenny knew that it would be Genevieve. Genevieve was relieved to learn that Jenny was there. "Now it will be all right," she said. "Enjoy yourself, darling, and remember to be at the bus station by four o'clock a week from today. Tell your dad you've got to be on time."

"Do you want something to eat?" Laura said, when Jenny hung up the phone.

"I'd better not," Jenny said. "The thing is, I threw up on the bus, and I'd better not eat anything yet."

Laura and Jenny's father were very concerned. Laura wanted to take her temperature, and her father wanted to call up a neighbor who was a nurse's aide.

"It's just motion sickness," Jenny said. "I always get sick when I ride in anything." So Jenny lay on the couch where she was going to sleep during her visit, and her father got a pillow and a soft quilt and covered her. He had a tired face and worried eyes, but he had a good smile, too, and when he put the cover over her, he kissed her forehead.

Then he and Laura sat on the floor in front of the couch, and they turned on the television. "This is nice," Jenny said drowsily. And even though she had been looking forward to watching television because theirs at home hadn't worked since before Christmas, she fell asleep in a few minutes.

(24)

"How's Linda?"

"Boy, is it hot today!"

"Would you like a coke?"

That was the only kind of thing her father said to her. Jenny didn't mind, though. She liked his square, solid shape, his thin, carefully combed hair, his strong arms, and his deep voice. She even liked his not knowing what to say to her.

Mr. Reed had had many different jobs, which made Jenny think that he must be very smart. He got up at five o'clock in the morning because he worked the early shift. He never woke Jenny or Laura when he left.

One evening the three of them went to a movie. It was a children's movie that Laura and Jenny's dad thought she would like. Jenny thought that the movie was loud and boring, but she enjoyed the theater, the popcorn machine, and the crowd of people. Once, long ago, there had been a movie theater in Crooked Creek, but now the building was a furniture store. Sometimes there were movies in the Episcopal Church basement, and Jenny never missed one, but this was more fun, even if she didn't like the film.

And sitting there with her own father was strangely wonderful. Daddy, she let herself think. My dad.

When school started, she thought with pleasure, and everyone wanted to know what she had done during the summer, she would be able to say, "I visited my dad in Indianapolis."

And would she visit him again? Ever again? Jenny pushed the question away. I'm here now, she thought. I'm really here.

Laura was between jobs, and the next day she took Jenny to a big shopping center. At first, Jenny loved it. There was a fountain in the middle, and lots of enormous plants, and so many stores full of pretty things. Very soon, though, she got tired. She hadn't realized that they were going into every single store. "Haven't we already been in this one?" she asked. That store seemed to be selling exactly the same shirts and jeans and purses as all the others. But Laura hurried in. She tried on dresses and necklaces. She opened up umbrellas and fingered scarves. She didn't buy anything. At long last, Laura decided that they should stop shopping and have a snack in a wildly decorated ice-cream shop. Jenny wanted lemonade, but Laura insisted that she have a big sundae that cost a fortune.

Laura sipped iced tea and watched Jenny try to eat the sundae, which was called the Tropical Hoosier Paradise. It had only a little ice cream in it. Mostly it was canned fruit and imitation whipped cream. Jenny didn't like it; she even hated it. Laura kept watching her, though, so she tried to eat what she could.

"I'm not really used to things like this," she said finally. "I'm sorry, but I can't finish it." Mainly she was sorry about the money that had been spent on it.

"It was so much fun to watch you enjoy that sundae!" Laura said, as they left the ice-cream store.

(25)

One evening Jenny's dad drove her past the factory where he worked. "It's as big as Crooked Creek!" she said. But so ugly, she thought.

"I wish I could see Crooked Creek again," her dad said.

"You should come! It isn't really very far."

"I don't think so."

"I don't see why," Jenny said sadly. For a minute, she had imagined herself and her dad walking around Crooked Creek, stopping by to say hello to everyone, maybe going out to the state park.

"For one thing, I don't think they like me out there."

"Nobody says that!" Jenny said. "Hardly anyone even mentions you."

"That's what I mean."

After a little while, he said, "That was my home. Nearly all my life."

He seemed so sad that Jenny wanted to cheer

him up. "But now you have your nice apartment," she said. "There's nothing like that in Crooked Creek. And Mr. Rudolf said to remember him to you. I forgot to tell you."

Her father just nodded.

"How is your mother?" he asked in a formal way, as if "your mother" were someone he had never met.

Jenny wanted to say, "She's lonely!" She wanted to say, "We worry about her because she hardly ever goes out of the apartment except to go to work. And Miss Golf is nasty to her and makes her work extra and doesn't give her any extra pay. And Mom doesn't go to church anymore, or out to play cards.

"She doesn't call anyone up, and now it seems like hardly anyone calls her up, either, except Genevieve. She doesn't save recipes anymore, or have plants, or sew. She doesn't go to open house at the school, or to the PTA. She doesn't even ask about school. She doesn't write to Mary Ellen's parents, even though they write to her, and she liked them so much. And she doesn't smile. She

doesn't ever smile. I'm so worried about her, Daddy,
I'm so worried!"

"How's your mother?" her father asked again
because she hadn't answered.

"She's okay," Jenny said, and that was all.

(26)

"What about your sister?" Laura asked one day.

"Linda? She's fine. She's working in Bloomington this summer. She has a good job at the university."

"We'd like to see her sometime. We don't have her address, though."

"I can give it to you."

"I never remember things like that," Laura said.

"I'll write it down for you if you'll tell me where to find a pencil."

"Oh, do it later, honey. There's no rush. I can't think where to find a pencil right now."

Later Jenny found a pencil and wrote down Linda's address. She gave it to her dad, who looked at it for a long time. Then he folded it and put it in his pocket.

Laura let Jenny cook all she wanted to while she was there. "I like to cook," Jenny said, "and this is such a nice kitchen."

"Well, good," Laura said, "because I hate cooking. I hate the mess, and nothing ever turns out right."

"Dave, my friend in Crooked Creek, says when you cook something good, it's like doing a painting or something."

"You're kidding," Laura said. "What does he mean by that?"

"It's hard to explain," Jenny said. Impossible to explain to someone like Laura, she thought. But Laura was okay. They had a good time. Jenny looked at a lot of Laura's magazines. Some of them were mostly pictures of clothes, and some were about TV and movie stars, and some were love stories that Jenny had to laugh at a little because they were really silly, but she read them, anyway. They didn't have those on the bookmobile.

(28)

When Laura and Mr. Reed asked Jenny if there was anything special she wanted to do while she was in Indianapolis, she told them about the Soldiers and Sailors Monument and John Dillinger's grave. They seemed surprised. It turned out that they never went downtown where the Soldiers and Sailors Monument was, and they never went to Crown Hill Cemetery where John Dillinger was buried. There was plenty to do, though, and before she knew it, the visit was over.

Jenny's dad took her to the bus. Laura said good-bye at the apartment. "I'm so glad you came," Laura said. "Your dad wanted to see you so much. So did I. I knew we'd get along.

"Maybe you'll come back some time," she added.

Not *maybe*, Jenny thought. *I'm coming back!*

When they got to the bus station, they went straight to the bus and found Genevieve standing beside it in anguish. She was surrounded by even more shopping bags than she had arrived with.

"I thought you weren't going to make it!" she gasped. "Most people are already on the bus, and it's about to leave! We've got to get on!"

"Hello, Genevieve," said Jenny's father.

"Hello, Joe," said Genevieve. "I would have liked to talk to you, Joe, but we have to go."

Mr. Reed hugged Jenny. As the bus pulled away, she heard him shouting to her. "Jenny!" he called.

She strained to hear what he was saying.

"I would have driven you by the Monument," he said. "The Soldiers and Sailors Monument! But there wasn't enough time. I would have done it, though!"

"It's okay," Jenny said, but in a whisper. She had no energy. Could I be carsick already, she wondered. She slumped back in the seat and put her head on Genevieve's shoulder. Genevieve patted her hand. Jenny's mind seemed to shut off. She just listened to the bus noises as if there were nothing else in the world.

Not until the road began to rise and curve again as the bus headed south did she remember that she was going home, and that was good.

Mrs. Reed was standing in front of Genevieve's Restaurant waiting for the bus. Maybe Jenny didn't really look at her mother very often, because she was surprised to see how nice her mother looked. She's even a little pretty! Jenny thought.

Jenny had never gone away before, and things did seem different. For the first time, she noticed how badly the restaurant needed to be painted. She noticed, too, that the twins, who came out to help Genevieve and her shopping bags off the bus, were men, not boys. Most of all, she was surprised at her mother. Then she realized that she had hardly ever seen her mother look really happy before.

"I'm so glad you came back," Mrs. Reed said.

"But you knew I was coming back," Jenny said. Her mother held her tight. "I never know anything for sure," she said.

"I might visit him again. He said so."

Her mother didn't say anything right away. Then

she said, "Maybe you can, honey. But right now I'm so glad you're back with me."

When she got home, she found that a postcard had come from Ellery. It said:

> Dear Jenny and her mother,
>
> This place gets rottoner every year. The conslers are grotesk. There is no food at all. Have a good summer.
>
> Your friend,
> Ellery Aldrich

(30)

The next morning, Jenny went to the house on the hill to see how it looked after her travels. It looked wonderful—quiet and peaceful and friendly. It would be a perfect house for parties. Birthday parties, Christmas Eve parties, Fourth of July picnics, brunches, barbecues . . . probably a party every week, all year round.

In between the parties, the family would be at home together, working on projects, talking things over. There would be no arguments. Everyone would have to help with the work, but everyone would want to. It was a house to be shared. If only there were someone to share it with . . . .

"Let's go for a walk," Jenny's mother said after supper that evening. Jenny was glad, for Mrs. Reed usually liked to stay at home. First they walked past a lot of stores so they could look at the interesting things in the windows. They read the sign on McCoy's door. It said, "I should be back some time this week."

Then they went up the hill. Jenny's mother liked the old houses, too. "I wonder who'll move in here," Mrs. Reed said, when they came to Jenny's house. "I always liked this one."

"Oh, I hope no one does!" Jenny said.

"Why?"

Jenny didn't know what to say.

"It isn't good for a house to sit empty," Mrs. Reed said. "They start to deteriorate. This is a pretty one. I hope somebody buys it soon."

Just then they heard horrible noises at the end of the block. Cautiously they walked toward Miss

Golf's house, where the noises were coming from.

Miss Golf kept two dogs. They were locked in a pen all the time, and they were big and ferocious-looking. Genevieve sometimes referred to Miss Golf and her dogs as "the triplets." Although they were not friendly dogs, they ordinarily kept quiet. At that moment, though, they were leaping in the air and yelping as if they were fighting off an invasion. Jenny and her mother looked around for the cause of it all. All they could see was a tiny, thin kitten who was standing near the pen gazing at the dogs. He held up his tail proudly and didn't budge.

"Look at that," Mrs. Reed said. "You old fools!" she shouted at the dogs.

Just then a window of Miss Golf's house was thrown open, and Miss Golf leaned out of it.

"What are you doing out there, Betty Reed? Those are very valuable dogs, and you're not to disturb them!"

"Your silly dogs are afraid of a kitten!" Mrs. Reed said, and to Jenny's amazement, she picked up the little cat and walked away as fast as she could. Jenny hurried after her. The kitten, who apparently thought nothing of being snatched away in this manner, began to purr loudly.

"Good for you!" Mrs. Reed said. "Standing up to those monsters! Look at his tail, Jenny."

Jenny saw that the end of the kitten's tail was missing.

"He must have seen a lot of trouble," Mrs. Reed said. "He looks terrible. No one's been taking care of him."

"Are you taking him home?" Jenny asked. Mrs. Reed slowed down. "I don't know," she said. "Maybe it wouldn't be a good idea." The kitten lifted his head and rubbed it against her cheek. "But it seems to me," she said, "that we ought to have him, and he ought to have us!"

"I think so, too!" Jenny said. "I know Mr. Rudolf won't mind."

"He won't," Jenny's mother said, "but I wonder about Albert."

"Oh." It was hard to imagine Albert putting up with another cat.

"It could be a problem," Jenny's mother said. "We'll just have to hope."

Jenny waited in front of the house with the kitten while her mother went in to talk to Mr. Rudolf. The kitten settled in her arms peacefully as if he had always known and loved her. In a minute, Mr. Rudolf and her mother came outside.

"Albert is just waking up from a little nap," Mr. Rudolf said after he had admired the little cat. "I think we should take the kitten in there and let Albert have a look at him. He never has cared much for cats, but maybe he'll tolerate this one."

Albert was in the rocking chair yawning, but when they brought the kitten into the room, he sat up at once and opened his eyes wide. Jenny put the kitten on the floor. He sat down in front of Albert's chair. He purred.

Albert looked sad, disappointed, and disgusted. He glared at Mr. Rudolf and meowed several times in a hoarse, quavering voice. Then he turned his back on them and lay down again.

"I think it will be all right," Mr. Rudolf said. "At any rate, he isn't going to absolutely forbid it." So Henry got to stay.

(32)

The next day Jenny went to Genevieve's Restaurant just long enough to tell Genevieve that she couldn't leave Henry that day. "It's his first day with us," she said. "I want to make sure he knows he belongs to us."

Genevieve had already heard about Henry. "You probably couldn't get him to leave now if you wanted to," she said. "I never could see much in cats." But she gave Jenny some bits of chicken in a little gravy to take to him. Henry was delighted. Jenny played with him in the yard most of the day except during his long naps, and she took him to visit Dave. She didn't get to the house on the hill, but she already knew that Henry was perfect for it.

That evening, Mr. Rudolf, Jenny, and her mother were sitting on the porch with Henry, who was sleeping peacefully on Mrs. Reed's lap. Albert, who was sitting in the front window, was keeping a suspicious eye on all of them. And then a little orange car crammed with people and duffle bags pulled up in front of the house and Jenny's sister Linda got out. The car pulled away and Linda ran grinning to the porch.

They all had to hug her and tell her how thin she was. Linda had turned beautiful, Jenny thought, since she was home last.

"What is *that*?" Linda asked, pointing at Henry.

"Our kitten," Mrs. Reed said.

"Just what you needed!" Linda said.

"I'm so glad you're here," Mrs. Reed said. "But how could you get a whole week off when it's only a summer job?"

"I asked," Linda said. "I said I would like a little time off to see my family. It can be done, you know. People do get time off. People who work in normal jobs, that is."

Jenny's mother looked annoyed. "I hope you didn't come home just to argue with me about my job," she said. "Anyway, I did take a day off not long ago. To help Jenny get ready to go to Indianapolis. She visited your dad."

Linda stared. "I'll have to hear about that," she said. They talked about other things, though, until the mosquitos got so bad that they had to go in.

"Where's the cat's litter box?" Linda asked them when they went upstairs.

Jenny and her mother hadn't thought about a litter box.

"There has to be a litter box," Linda said. "And do you understand that the cat will have to go to the vet? Can you afford it?"

"It couldn't cost much," Mrs. Reed said.

"It will cost a lot," Linda said firmly. "Maybe twenty-five or thirty dollars." This would be a big problem.

"Are you sure he has to go to the vet?" Jenny asked.

"Absolutely," Linda said. "He's got to have shots, and he's got to be neutered. And he's a stray, and you have to make sure he's healthy. Ask Mr. Rudolf if you don't believe me."

"I believe you." Mrs. Reed sighed. "But maybe we can manage. Jenny, could we wait a little longer to have the TV fixed? I know it's been a long time . . . ."

"Sure! I'd much rather have Henry!" Jenny said.

"Well, get him to the vet tomorrow," Linda said, "before we catch something from him. I'll get a litter box for you."

"Oh, Linda, you're so nice! And you don't even like cats!" Jenny said.

"I don't like cats, and I especially don't like *this* ridiculous cat, but if you two want him, you are going to have him, and I don't want to hear any more about it."

33

When Henry came back from the vet, Jenny and her mother gave him a bath. Albert looked on. It was a terrible experience for everyone. After Henry was dried off, though, he was fluffy and fragrant and a better color.

"He'll be a handsome animal some day," Mr. Rudolf said. "And in the meantime, he certainly has character."

Linda stayed for a week. She polished everything that could be polished, rearranged the cupboards, tightened the doorknobs, fixed the dripping faucets. She dusted lampshades, cleaned out the refrigerator, painted the kitchen cabinets. She washed the curtains and shampooed the living-room rug. She made a new sundress for Jenny and one for Mrs. Reed. "Now put them on and go somewhere!" she said crossly.

While Linda worked, she lectured, telling Jenny and her mother that they were not keeping up with things, not seeing enough people, not eating enough fresh food. Jenny wondered why she was so happy to have Linda nagging at her again.

Linda slept on the couch, and Henry slept on her feet. Early each morning he walked up her legs and over her stomach and then stood on her chest and stared at her until she got up and fed him. Late each afternoon, Linda took time to go to see Dave at the Art Center. Perhaps over there she sat down, Jenny thought. At least she was in a good mood when she came back.

One evening Jenny's mother was wondering, as she often did, whether to color her hair so the gray wouldn't show. Jenny liked her mother's hair the way it was.

Jenny's mother thought she ought to lose some weight. Jenny thought her mother's weight was fine.

Jenny's mother wished she could think of the right things to say to people. Jenny thought she usually did say the right things.

Linda said that her mother should color her hair, lose ten pounds, learn to speak up for herself, and find a better job. She said that she would make a list of the subjects Mrs. Reed should study at the night classes for adults. She said that it would be a long list.

Mrs. Reed looked from one of them to the other. "Oh, well," she said.

"Who do you spend your time with, now that Mary Ellen's gone?" Linda asked.

"There aren't many kids around this summer," Jenny said.

"Where are little Hickory and Dickory?"

"If you mean Hilary and Ellery, they're at camp."

"What do you do all the time?"

"I help Genevieve and talk to Dave and Mr. Rudolf . . . and stuff. You know, I just wander around."

"I wish there were more kids around."

"It doesn't matter. Don't worry about it." Jenny longed to tell Linda about the house, and show it to her, but she decided she'd better not. After all, Linda was an adult now.

"Mom should be home with you more in the summer," Linda said.

"But it's the busy season . . . ."

"Oh, I know. Heaven forbid that Greta Golf should sell one bar less of hand-painted soap! Maybe I should have come home this summer, but

I couldn't have gotten a decent job here. And I like it in Bloomington."

"Why do you worry about us? We get along all right."

"You don't get along all right! You live in this little closet, and you don't go anywhere. It isn't good for either one of you!"

"Oh, Linda, shut up about it!" Jenny said.

Surprisingly, Linda did.

Jenny had had all she could take of home-improvement and self-improvement for a while, so she gathered up Henry and took him to the house on the hill. As far as she was concerned, not one thing needed to be changed there.

She hadn't brought Henry to the house before, although she had wanted to badly. After that day, she never brought him back again, for she almost lost him there as he ran wildly through the empty rooms, up and down the stairs, hiding under radiators and getting all sooty in the fireplaces.

"I wish we could come here and stay," she said to him when she finally captured him, "but I'm afraid this will be your last visit."

36

"What are you doing that for?" Jenny asked Linda another afternoon. Linda was doing something to a window shade she had taken down.

"So it'll work, silly! Doesn't it drive you crazy having things that don't work right?"

"No," Jenny said. "We never close it, anyway. Come on, let's go sit down on the porch." But Linda was too busy.

"If I keep at it," she said, "I can have this place all organized for you by the time I leave."

"Oh, good," Jenny said. "I was afraid there might be some little crumb somewhere you'd miss."

"I suppose I should ask . . ." Linda said after a while.

"Yes?"

"So, how was the daddy?"

"He's nice, Linda. He's really nice. He wants you to come and see him, too."

"I'll bet," Linda said.

"He does! He said so. So did Laura."

"Okay, okay," Linda said. "Did he meet you at the bus? Or did he forget?"

"He met me. He was a little late, but he met me. They live in a really nice apartment."

"And what about her?"

"She's okay. She looks fairly pretty. She has pretty clothes. Only she seems . . . ."

"How does she seem?"

"She seems like the kind of person you never get to know, no matter how much time you spend with her."

"I doubt if there's really much to know. Did you have a good time there?"

"Yes," Jenny said. "I'm glad I went. He says he wants both of us to come and see him next summer."

For once, Linda stopped working and looked straight into Jenny's eyes. "Where would I get the time or money to go to Indianapolis?" she asked. "And how do I know he'd even be there if I did go?"

Jenny didn't want to think about that question.

Finally she said, "He gave me some money to get a sweater for school."

"Big deal!" Linda said. "She ought to make him send some money. But she won't stand up for herself."

"Linda," Jenny said, hearing with surprise how strong and determined her own voice sounded, "I'm going back, when I can."

After a minute, Linda said, "Suit yourself." Then she suddenly pulled down the window shade she had been working on. It rolled itself up to the top of the window with a bang. "I'm going to wash my hair," she said.

Jenny longed to go over to the house on the hill, where there was no one to ask her questions. But it was too risky. Better to wait until Linda went back to Bloomington.

(37)

Linda went back to college Friday morning, and the weekend seemed to last forever.

"Why can't we get a movie theater in this town?" Jenny's mother demanded on Sunday afternoon. "There isn't anything to do—not even housework because Linda's got everything so clean. And I don't have anything to read because I missed the bookmobile again. And it's hot. And I didn't want Linda to go."

"I know," Jenny said. "Well, they say there may be a movie in the new shopping center someday. And they say there may be a swimming pool at the school someday, and . . ."

"Someday's going to be too late for me," Mrs. Reed said. Then she brightened up and said something that surprised Jenny. "Maybe Willy Rudolf could come up for supper tonight," she said. "We could have the rest of the cold ham, and I could make biscuits. I'll ask him."

Jenny couldn't remember when they had had company for a meal—except Ellery, of course—and she was pleased.

But Mr. Rudolf was going to the Historical Society's annual picnic at the state park, so he couldn't come.

"Oh, well," Mrs. Reed said. "I'm so desperate I may have to look at that list of classes Linda wants me to take." She started to go into the bedroom, and then she came back. "I've been thinking . . ." she said.

"Yes?"

"You must wonder what happened with your dad and me."

"Yes, I do," Jenny said.

"Someday we'll talk about it," Mrs. Reed said softly. "I can see that we ought to." She put her arms around Jenny. "You and Linda are such good kids," she said. "I've felt bad because you couldn't have the nice things I wanted for you."

"It doesn't matter . . ." Jenny began, but her mother interrupted.

"It matters!" she said. "But when I see how well Linda is doing—how she decides what she wants and figures out how to get it—then I see that things can change."

Mrs. Reed went into the bedroom, and in a minute she came back with Linda's list. She sat down to read it, and every once in a while she laughed.

"What's so funny?"

"Linda's list. She wants to make me over. Listen to these classes: 'Makeovers for the Middle-aged'; 'Building Self-Confidence'; 'Getting Organized for the Hopelessly Confused'; 'Dance Yourself Thin'; 'Veggies for Vitality.' And that's just for this fall. She's got half a dozen more for me to take in the winter."

It occurred to Jenny that not long ago, her mother probably would have been crying instead of laughing at the thought that Linda didn't approve of her just the way she was.

"It's a good list," her mother said.

"You mean you're going to go to the classes?"

"No. I have something else I want to do instead. While you were gone, Dave told me about a Career Center that's going to open up at the high school in September. It's for adults, and it's free. They have all kinds of information about jobs and about what you have to study to get the jobs. They help you figure out what you'd be good at. The person in charge of it is a friend of Dave's. He's already talked to her, and she's going to send me some booklets to look at, so I can go over as soon as it opens."

"That sounds good, Mom!"

"But don't tell anyone!" Mrs. Reed said. "Not even Genevieve! Because I don't want Greta Golf to hear about it until I've talked to those people at the center. And don't tell Linda! Because if it falls through . . . ."

"It won't fall through," Jenny said, "but I won't tell anybody, don't worry." Then she went happily outside, while her mother dug out some mending Linda hadn't found out about.

(38)

Jenny decided to go to the house on the hill. She hadn't visited the house since the time she had taken Henry there, and now she could hardly wait to get back to it. She noticed that the grass had been cut, and the walks were swept clean. How pretty it was, even nicer than she had remembered. She wondered how many other kids it had welcomed in the hundred years or more since it was built.

Jenny went to the back of the house and, as usual, she pushed gently on the basement window. It swung in easily, and she slid down the wall, landing comfortably. Then she hurried up the basement stairs, and—the door at the top of the stairs wouldn't open.

Jenny just couldn't believe it. She turned the knob and turned it, but the door didn't budge. She pushed with all her strength, but that didn't help. The door was bolted. Jenny's hands were damp, and her heart pounded. Someone had been in her house and had locked the basement door. She couldn't get in. And what was more, how would she get out of the basement again? She hurried back down the stairs and looked up at the window. It looked very high. She tried to pull herself up to it, but her sandals were slippery, and there was nothing to get a grip on.

It was important to be calm, but it was going to be very hard. No—it was going to be impossible! Nobody knew where she was, and she had no way of getting out! Maybe she would starve, or maybe someone would catch her here. They might call the sheriff! She had to get out! Again she tried to scramble up to the window, but she only scraped her arms and legs on the rough wall.

Then she heard a noise. It was the sound of a car in the driveway. Doors slammed, and Jenny heard voices, lots of them. Then she heard footsteps above her head. "Oh, no," she whispered. She squeezed as close as possible to the wall. If she was perfectly quiet, maybe they wouldn't know she was there.

But how long would they stay? Who were they? Had someone bought the house—or was it the police? Would they think she was a juvenile delinquent? *Was* she a juvenile delinquent?

Jenny tried never to cry, but she couldn't help it now. How loud the footsteps were! It sounded like an army tramping through the house. Why had she ever come inside? It was a stupid thing to do. Stupid!

The door at the top of the stairs opened so quickly that it was like an explosion. Then a big boy clattered down the stairs carrying a large box. Jenny didn't even breathe, but the boy was coming right toward her. All at once, he saw her, and his mouth dropped open. For a few seconds, they stared at each other. Then he dropped the box and ran wildly back up the stairs, yelling, "Dad! Dad! There's someone in the basement!"

It was only seconds before the ceiling light went on, and there were more people coming down the steps. They were all looking at her. The big boy was jumping around excitedly; the others just looked surprised. There were a man and a woman and three more children.

When they saw Jenny, the children began to smile a little, but the man and woman looked furious.

"How did you get in here?" the man demanded in a deep, loud voice. His face was red with anger, and he looked huge and mean.

Jenny pointed at the window. She was too frightened to talk.

"You know you don't belong in here!" the man said. Then the woman came nearer.

"But what did you want?" she asked.

Jenny had to clear her throat several times before any words came out. When she spoke, it was in a tiny voice she remembered as having belonged to her when she was about five years old.

"I just like coming here," she said.

"You mean you've been here before?"

"Quite a few times," Jenny whispered.

"Well, obviously she hasn't bothered anything," the woman said finally.

"Who are you, and where do you live?" asked the man, who was still angry.

"I'm Jennifer Reed, and I live over on Main Street," Jenny said reluctantly. "I didn't bother anything," she added. "I just liked the house."

"Okay," said the woman. "It's all right. You did surprise us, though, and you shouldn't have come in here like that. What if you'd had some kind of accident? No one would have known where to look for you. I'll bet your parents don't know you come in here, do they?"

"No." How foolish she had been, Jenny thought. How awful she must seem to them.

"Don't worry about it anymore," the woman said. "We've bought this house. We're going to move in next weekend. Our name is Branagan." She pointed to the big boy. "This is Ted." Then she introduced the other children: Amy, Tim, and Sarah. Amy was the one with braces on her teeth. Tim and Sarah were little and plump. All of them had friendly, curious brown eyes which made Jenny feel better.

"I wonder if you and Amy will be going to the same school," said Mrs. Branagan.

Amy smiled a huge smile. "Come on, Jenny," she said. "Let's go and find a Kleenex." They went upstairs, and all the children looked through boxes until they found some Kleenex. Jenny blew her nose for such a long time that she and Amy began to laugh and couldn't stop. Then they cleaned up Jenny's skinned knees and arms.

"Why don't you show me around the place now?" Amy asked. "I'm sure you know much more about it than I do!" This seemed funny, too, and so did everything else either one of them said for the next hour. Jenny was worn out with laughing and climbing stairs.

"This is more than I've laughed all summer," she said. "Ever since Mary Ellen moved away, I never seem to laugh anymore. She was my best friend. I can't even remember when I didn't know her."

"I know what you mean," Amy said. "When I found out that we had to move away from Cincinnati, I felt terrible. I think I'm going to like Crooked

Creek. I like the hills, and I love these old houses. Do you live in an old house, too?"

"Yes, but ours is little, and we only live in part of it. There's only my mother and me and our cat Henry at home now. I have a sister, but she's away at college."

"Where's your dad?"

"He lives in Indianapolis. I visited him this summer. Anyway, Mom and I live upstairs in our house, and Mr. Rudolf, who is eighty years old and very nice, lives downstairs."

"We're probably going to make an apartment in our house, too," Amy said, "on the third floor. We're going to do the work ourselves. We're all very handy."

"Why is your family moving to Crooked Creek?" Jenny asked. "Are you artists?"

"No. My dad's going to be superintendent of schools for the county. And Mom's going to teach, if she can get a job. They looked at houses in a lot of towns around here, but this is the one they wanted. Daddy grew up in a house like this, and he loves it.

He *is* nice, you know," Amy said anxiously. "Even a superintendent of schools can be nice."

"Oh, I'm sure he is. But I sure got off to a bad start with him."

"He'll get over it."

"Where are you, kids?" Mrs. Branagan called from downstairs. When she found them, she said, "Jenny, we brought a picnic supper with us for tonight. Would you like to eat with us?"

Jenny couldn't believe it. Could it have been only a couple of hours ago that she had been so bored?

"I'd love to," she said.

She called her mother to explain that she wouldn't be coming home for supper, and then she went with Amy and Ted to get the picnic things from the car.